To Take

A novella penned by:

PASSION FLOWS DEEPER THROUGH HER PEN

www.authorblove.com

Blessings list – www.crosswalk.org
Pastor's prayer – www.proverbs31.org
Maarz's prayer – www.togetherforlifeonline.com

For information about bulk purchases, please contact B. Love via email – authorblove@gmail.com

To join my mailing list and be the first to know about my latest releases click this link right here -> http://eepurl.com/bYzdcr

Interested in having your book published under B. Love Publications? Send the first three chapters of your manuscript to blovepublications@gmail.com with Submission as your subject.

Heeeyyyyy!

Okay, so, this won't be the traditional romance I'm sure you're used to reading... but close your eyes, take a deep breath, and ride this wave – only if you have an imagination. I needed a break from the norm, and since you and I are practically besties because you read my books I figured I'd force you to take a break too.

If you're looking for a realistic romance or a story packed with drama this is *NOT* the novella for you. Just don't even try to read it. Seriously. It's straight up unrealistic love at first sight, super sweet, and passionate romance. You've been warned. At the end... leave a review and tell me how much you liked it. ;)

Picture bride –

The term **picture bride** refers to the practice in the early 20th century of **immigrant** workers (chiefly **Japanese, Okinawan,** and **Korean**) in **Hawaii** and the **West Coast** of the **United States** and **Canada** selecting brides from their native countries via a **matchmaker,** who paired bride and groom using only photographs and family recommendations of the possible candidates. This is an abbreviated form of the traditional matchmaking process, and is similar in a number of ways to the concept of the **mail-order bride**.

This was the day I'd been avoiding for the past twenty-two years of my life. Okay, well maybe not the *entire* twenty-two years, but like... 10. See, I live in a small town that has basically overlooked the fact that arranged marriages are no longer necessary. I live in a small town that doesn't believe in allowing people to choose their own paths for love and life. They believe your mate for life determines the success or failure of your life. Because of that, they choose your marriage partner for you.

For women like me... women who choose to stay after high school instead of running for the hills... we were lucky enough to get through high school and college before being married off, but I knew once I crossed the stage and grabbed my diploma that my day would be coming soon.

This was the day.

I stepped outside to go to the store and crushed a box that was left in front of my door. After having a little life scared out of me and cursing loud enough to make my next door neighbor's dog shriek and run away, I leaned down and grabbed the box. There was no name on the box – just the customary white ribbon symbolizing it was my betrothal box.

The box that my parents had been waiting to give me for years.

The inside of this box held the picture of the man I was going to be married to, all of his background and family information, a letter from him, and our wedding date. As I took the box back into my small cottage home I couldn't help but think about the fact that I had an out and didn't take it.

On my eighteenth birthday I had the option of leaving Crimson Trails or staying. My ass chose to stay. I guess it's really not *that* bad here. My best friends are here and I adore them. My parents are here and I want to please them and pay them back for all they've given me. My marriage would be my way of doing so. Not only did my future husband or his family have to pay a pretty hefty betrothal fee to secure our marriage, but it would be on me and his shoulder's to take care of my parents when they decided to retire.

About ninety-eight percent of the arranged marriages lasted, and for the most part all of the married couples seemed fairly happy, so I figured it wouldn't be too bad. But now that the time had come... that *my* time had come... eh.

As I took the crushed box back into my home I considered calling my besties but it would be pointless. Trevena was working as a paralegal while going to grad school to become a lawyer. Chrisette had her own beauty salon. And me? I write for the towns newspaper and magazine. I also write eBooks under a pen name because if my parents knew the type of shit I was writing about they'd think I'd lost my damn mind!

My schedule is pretty flexible and I do a great deal of writing at home, so I usually end up having to wait until the evening to hang with my girls.

I placed the box on my kitchen table, put my hands on both sides of it, and stared at it — like that would make it magically open and reveal its contents to me.

"Just open it, Haylo," I ordered, only to ignore my own request.

Pacing back and forth didn't make this any easier. The only thing that could be heard in my kitchen was the sound of my shoes on the floor until my phone rang. I pulled it out of my pocket and smiled at the sight of my mother's picture.

"Hey, Momma."

"Hey, ladybug. Anything interesting happen today?"

With a smile and roll of my eyes, I returned to the table and stood in front of the box again.

"Yep. There was a package at my front door."

"Oh yea? What was it?"

"I can't say for sure because I haven't opened it yet, but it looks like a betrothal box."

"You don't say?"

"Momma!"

She chuckled and I unwillingly joined in with her.

"Open it, ladybug. We did good by you. I think you're going to be pleasantly surprised by who we chose for you."

"You promise? Is he ugly? *Please*, Momma…"

"Haylo, open the box. Stop by later and we'll talk."

Without waiting for me to agree, she hung up the phone and put me in the same position I was in before she called – scared out of my mind!

"Just open it and get it over with. It can't be that bad. If it was bad she would've sounded sad or worried. Just open it."

I placed my hands on top of the box, inhaled deeply and prayed before pulling the tape from around the top. Then the sides. I opened the box and my heart dropped. No. It skipped a beat. Sped up. Stopped. *Then* dropped.

"You have *got* to be kidding me."

Snatching the picture out of the box, I squealed and did a poor imitation of the running man and cabbage patch all in one. Homeboy was fine! No. Homeboy was fiinnnneeee!

His skin was the same brown as peanut butter.

Golden brown eyes. Really. They looked like pools of gold in the center. All bright and shiny and just… golden.

A stubbly beard lined his strong jaw.

He had pink full lips. The bottom one was just a tad bit bigger than the top one. So round. So full. *Yum.*

His eyebrows were thick and bushy.

And his nose was wide and manly.

With him wearing a sleeveless muscle shirt, I could see that he had at least one tattoo… and hair on the top of his chest.

Good God.

Hair never looked so sexy.

All I wanted to do was run my fingers through that hair.

I couldn't see the hair on his head, though, because he had on a hat that was on backwards. From the little that I could see it was in some type of low cut.

Yea, they did good by me.

Really good.

Shaking hands put the picture down only to replace it with his background and family sheet.

Maarz Henry

Son of Leo and Faye Henry
Younger brother to Bryson Henry
Age – 28
Birthday – May 1st
Height – 6'2
Weight – 170 lbs.
Education – Bachelor's degree in finance.
Occupation – Financial advisor at Henry & Sons Financial Institute
No major health issues to report.
No mental illness to report.

I tossed the sheet down with one hand and grabbed his letter with the other. Even his handwriting was neat and pretty. There had to be a catch, and I was quite frankly scared to find out what it was.

Haylo,

Such a beautiful name for a beautiful woman I'm sure. It's crazy how I've never seen or heard of you. As small as this town is you'd think I'd know everyone; especially with my career, but you, young lady, have successfully slid under my radar. That's cool. It just makes me all the more anxious to receive my box from you.

Do you know what your name means, beloved? Halo means divine aura. It represents holiness. It's symbolic of angels and the light of grace covering us by God.

You're my halo, Haylo, but I'm no angel... not all the time at least. And that's not to say I'm a bad guy. I'm... well you'll see. I won't get too deep with this first letter as we will have two months to write each other. This whole not being able to talk on the phone thing will drive me fucking crazy because I desperately want to hear you... see you... something. But I'll wait for your box patiently.

Until then,
Your husband – Maarz Henry

I could've turned into a puddle of mush and melted through the cracked tile on my floor. My husband. Maarz Henry. Maybe this won't be so bad after all.

MAARZ

This was the day I'd been waiting for for the past week. Haylo's box. My parents sat me down at 13 and told me my marriage was going to be arranged unless I left town. Now I will admit, I planned on leaving the second I graduated high school, but there was something inside of me that told me to stay.

There was something that told me to wait.

That what I left to gain might not be as good as what was here waiting for me.

So I stayed.

And waited.

And two weeks ago after years of waiting my parents told me that it was time.

The only thing they told me about my wife was her name and her parents name and occupation. Everything else I'd have to learn from her on our first meeting and after our wedding.

I put my beer on the coffee table and placed the box in my lap. The entire time I pulled the tape away I couldn't ignore the drumming of my heart. Rumbling in my stomach. Sweat forming under my armpits and on the palms of my hands. This woman was to be my wife, and I didn't know anything about her ass.

She was going to be my responsibility.

I was going to have to provide for her. Protect her. Lead her. Love her. Romance her. Be fruitful and multiply with her.

What if I didn't like her? What if she couldn't stand me? What if we didn't get along? None of that mattered at this point. The betrothal fee had been paid and our wedding date had already been selected.

As I opened the box my eyes opened and closed while I inhaled deeply. The first thing I saw was Haylo's picture... and she was gorgeous. Forget drop dead gorgeous; Haylo was *try to live forever to spend it with her* gorgeous.

She had the most beautiful honey brown skin I'd ever seen.

Her hair was thick, jet black, and shoulder length.

Almond shaped ebony eyes held me captive, until I took in her lips.

Her full, pink, juicy looking lips.

The shirt she had on had a low V cut, so I had no problem seeing the sides of her perky breasts.

Damn.

This was my wife?

What did I do to deserve such a gorgeous woman?

Her ass had to be crazy.

No way in hell she was single for no reason.

Unless the reason was she was being saved for me?

Still holding her picture in my left hand, I pulled her background sheet out with my right.

Haylo Dixon
Daughter of Phillip and Lucy Dixon
Older sister to Leigha Dixon
Age – 22
Birthday – August 23rd
Height – 5'3
Weight – It's impolite to ask this.
Education – Bachelor's degree in creative writing.
Occupation – Writer for both Crimson Trails Newspaper and Magazine
No major health issues to report.
No mental illness to report.

After stealing another long glance at her picture, I put it and her background sheet down to read her letter.

Maarz,

I'm writing this immediately after opening your box. I wanted to capture exactly how I feel in this moment. There's no doubt in my mind that my letters will always be longer than yours because I'm a writer, but I'll try not to bore you too much.

Hope this isn't too forward, but you're very handsome. As shallow as this may sound, that was my biggest fear. You looking like a pug or Bedlington terrier.

The hell was a Bedlington terrier? I grabbed my phone to look the dog up, and as soon as the pictures popped up I cracked up. This girl was going to be a trip.

I swear I'm not shallow, though. My parents assured me that they would choose a man that would be able to not only provide and protect, but complement my energy as well. Unlike a lot of parents, they took my happiness into consideration. So I'm confident that we'll get along just fine. There was just a matter of your face that I was concerned about. But I am very, very pleased.

Your letter was so sweet. Made me feel all… giddy. Like I felt going to my first B2K concert years ago. Hell, how I felt when we got our first ice cream slush shop last year! On my life, that is my most favorite thing to drink.

How should we do this? Should we get to know each other through these letters or face to face? I'm following your lead.

Can I bear my soul to you, Maarz? I'm so freaking scared. Like, what if you don't like me? What if I'm not your type? What if I can't please you? What if I can't cook the food you like? What if I can't please you sexually? I don't want you to be miserable for the rest of your life because of me. If you want to back out I will completely understand.

Just… if you do… do it before we meet please.

Your ~~wife~~ halo,
Haylo Dixon-Henry ;)

I wanted, no I *needed* to reassure her. I wanted to look her up, find her number, and call her. Tell her that she had nothing to worry about. That I was invested in this. In us. That she didn't have to worry about failing because we were going to figure this shit out together. Since I couldn't call her I did the only thing I could do – write her.

Haylo

Yo,

You have nothing to worry about, Haylo. I give you my word — I'm committed to making us work. Don't worry about failing because you won't. You don't have to worry about me not liking you; I already do. You're beautiful. You're silly I can already tell. You're creative and passionate about your writing.

Above all… you didn't come to me with a list of demands… your concern was pleasing me. Do you know how selfless that is? How sexy your submission is? Do you know how much that made me want to please you and take care of you? Trust me… we gon be alright, Haylo.

You are my type. That skin. Those eyes. Your lips. You are gorgeous, beloved. Gorgeous. There's not a thing about you that I would change. You will please me. Things won't be perfect between us all the time. We will have our highs and lows. Ima get on your nerves and you'll get on mine, but I'm sure we'll spend more time in love and peace than we will getting under each other's skin.

Can you cook? If you can't my mama will teach you. I'll eat just about anything as long as it's seasoned and not under or overcooked.

Sex is one thing you will never have to worry about. Ever. As long as you don't deny me of it I'll take care of the rest. I'll mold you and teach you whatever I want you to know. I'll take care of your body just as well as I'm going to take care of every other part of you. And pleasing you will please me.

I don't think there's anything about you that will make me miserable for the rest of my life. Maybe being away from you will and even that won't. It'll help me appreciate the time I do have with you. I'm not backing out, Haylo, and I hope you don't either. I'm actually looking forward to meeting you. Being with you. Marrying you. Is that crazy of me?

Tell me everything there is to know about you in your next letter. Don't leave anything out.

Ride with your man, baby. I got you.

Maarz

Chrisette snatched Maarz's letter from me and took off down the hall. She'd been trying to get me to open and read it to her since the mailman ran and I'd refused. I was anxious to read his letter, but I didn't want to read it while she was here. I was unsure of how he was going to answer my questions. Being turned down by him and dying of embarrassment in front of my best friend was not how I wanted to spend my Saturday afternoon. Racing behind her, I grabbed her by her ponytail and yanked her back to me.

"Give me my letter, Chris," I said a lot more calmly than I actually felt.

Call me possessive, but that was all I had of my man and I didn't want to share him with anyone else.

"Alright, alright. Strong grip ass."

Chrisette handed me the letter and followed me back into my living room. Today was one of the rare days that she didn't have any clients until later today, so she was meeting Trevena over here to get the details about Maarz. *Maarz*. Ugh. I couldn't even think about him without getting all smiley and googly eyed. And this letter just further made me feel infatuated with him. He had such a way with words, and words meant *everything* to me.

That has gotten me into trouble in the past. Dealing with little boys who tossed out words and promises without meaning them at all. Dealing with little boys who could never match their actions with their words.

I don't know, though, there was something about Maarz that seemed different. That seemed genuine.

"Do I really have to wait for Tre to get here? I already had to wait forever because our schedules have been conflicting. I want details!" Chrisette whined.

That was true. She had waited a *whole* 5 days to hear about Maarz and my box. Between her late nights at the shop and Trevena's workload because of the case she's helping with, we hadn't really had much time to kick it as usual.

"If I tell you you'll have to hear it all over again when Tre gets here."

"I don't mind."

"Fine. When I was leaving to go to the gro—"

Trevena rang the doorbell and stopped me before I got too deep in my spill. I got up to let her and the bottle of Remy Martin that she had in. We hugged and she did the same with Chrisette before we poured up and I finished telling them all about the box, Maarz's first letter, and now the second.

"Maarz Henry? Of Henry & Sons? That's who I let handle my money. Well not him, but their company. I think his brother is actually the one that's my accountant. Is his brother Bryson Henry?" Chrisette asked.

"Yep, that's them. So you've seen Maarz in person?"

"In passing. I've seen him a few times when I've gone up there, but we've never really talked."

"Is he as fine in person as he is in his picture?"

"Girl. Finer. We never talked mostly because when I was around him I couldn't do anything but stare and almost drool. He would always flash a sexy smile and speak to me before going to do whatever he was going to do."

"So we have to go up there, Chris! I wanna see him too," Trevena added.

"You can't see him and meet him before I do. It's bad enough that she has," I declined.

"Let me check him out for you, sis. Get a feel for him before you go through with this bullshit."

"Bullshit?" me and Chrisette repeated in unison.

"It's only bullshit because your parents haven't given you away yet," Chrisette continued. "Shoot I'll be glad when I'm chosen. As long as he looks half as good as Lolo's man does."

"Whatever, Chris. So you gon let me go up there or not, Lolo?"

Both sets of eyes were on me. I should've said no. I *really* should've said no. But instead I said...

"Fine, but don't let him see you. And *don't* embarrass me."

MAARZ

Maarz,

Tell you everything about me? Where would I begin? At the beginning? Like of my life? Okay, my name is Haylo Dixon. I'm twenty-two years old. Well you already know this stuff hehehe. Ummm I hate this if you can't tell. Let's see... oh! One thing that I'm super proud of is my job. I love writing.

I got an internship with Crimson Trails magazine my senior year of college, and when I graduated they hired me fulltime. I write for our newspaper as well. Something that no one knows about me is that I also write eBooks. Erotica eBooks. I've read so many romance novels, erotica novels, and watched so many chick flicks that I write them as if I actually know what I'm talking about.

Between my royalties and my salary, I was able to buy this cute little cottage by the lake. It's what I'm most proud of. I guess after we get married I'll have to move in with you, but I'm going to keep my cottage. It's already paid for. Maybe I'll use it as like a writing office or something. I don't know.

Besides writing I love eating, shopping, getting manicures and pedicures, and watching movies. I really enjoy fishing too. Strange I'm sure, but I do. That's another reason I got this cottage is because I like to get up early on Saturday mornings, head out to my boat, and just sit on the water until my best friends come over.

I have two – Trevena and Chrisette. We've been besties since grade school. I'm really close to my family. What else?

My favorite color is pink. I'm a girly girl, but I love sports and trap music. My favorite artist is Tupac. I ain't no killa but don't push me! That's legit my life. My first year of high school you wouldn't believe how much I was picked on because of my looks. Jealousy is a motherfucker. They left me alone after my besties and I tagged a few asses, though.

Favorite food is chicken. Or maybe pasta. Least favorite food is... I can't think of one.

I hate when people lie. I hate when people can't communicate. I hate inconsistency. I love love. I love romance. I love long talks about nothing. I love silence that says everything.

I don't like talking about myself, Maarz. I want to know about you. I wish I could talk to you. Hear your voice. I wanna know how you smell. Do you have a signature cologne? I bet your natural scent is everything. You look like you smell like a man. Is that weird? You just look like you smell... I don't know. Like you look. Lol. Creep moment – I sleep with your picture taped to my pillow. TMI? Lord. I'm probably scaring you away. I'm not crazy, Maarz, I swear. I'm just going to stop this letter now!

Haylo

I didn't realize how hard I was smiling until I covered my mouth with my hand and shook my head. So she wants to know how I smell? We can make that happen. It would be against Crimson Trails betrothal law for me to call her, but I'd never been one that followed all the rules. Knowing damn well that I shouldn't, I looked up our local newspaper's website and found their list of writers.

Haylo was at the top of the list along with her email and phone number. After locking her number into my phone I stood and headed out of my office.

"Mr. Henry, don't forget you have a three o'clock meeting," the office assistant, Erica, reminded me.

"Thanks, E."

I nodded at the two women that were seated by the front door before going out. One I recognized as one of our clients, the other I didn't. They both were sitting there staring at me with wide ass grins on their faces. That was something I was used to, though. It used to boost my ego, but now that I was looking forward to spending my life with Haylo it didn't faze me at all.

Once I was in my car I pulled her number back up and called her. Two rings in she answered. I froze at the sound of her voice. She sounded so good. Her voice was low. Soft. Smooth. Like honey. Like her skin. Just hearing her say hello had me wondering how she'd sound moaning in my ear.

"Is this..." her voice raised just slightly in excitement. I could literally hear the smile in her voice. "Maarz?"

"Yea, it's me. I know I shouldn't have called but..."

Her squeal into the phone cut off my words and made me chuckle.

"Is this really you? How do I know it's really you?"

"Do you want me to FaceTime you?"

"God you sound you good. You sound better than I thought you would."

"Shit, Haylo. You can't be saying stuff like that. I already fucked up by calling you. You gon make me mess around and come see you."

"Well what do you want me to say, babe? I was hoping you'd call me. I really wanted to hear you. Thank you so much."

"You don't have to thank me for this. I've been wanting to call you too. Wanting to hear you. See you. Feel you," shaking those desires out of my head I beat it against the headrest gently, "I uh... I'm about to head to the house and put something together for you. You should get it in about two days."

"Okay. Maarz?"

"Yea, baby?"

"You don't know how happy you just made me."

With a smile I started my car and pulled out of the parking lot.

"I do, because hearing your voice has made me happy too."

Haylo

This was the biggest package I'd gotten from Maarz so far and I couldn't wait to see what was inside! Ever since his random call I haven't heard from him. As much as I didn't want to, we agreed that that would be the only time we talked on the phone, but damn I wanted his voice to put me to sleep.

Finding enough self-discipline that I didn't even know I had, I was able to finish my articles for the day and get about ten thousand words written on my next novel before I scurried into the living room to open his package.

At the top of the package was a t-shirt that smelled like him. Like *him*. I couldn't resist pulling the shirt to my nose and inhaling his hypnotic scent. Under the shirt was a DVD of my favorite movie, *Poetic Justice*, a bag of popcorn, and a one-hundred-dollar gift card to Creamed – my most favorite ice cream slush shop! How sweet was he? Last but most definitely not least was his letter.

Mrs. Henry,

There's so much I want to say to your sexy sounding ass I don't even know where to start. I guess the box that I'm sending is a good place to start. You wanted to know how I smell? Now you do. I want you to sleep in that shirt. It'll make me feel like I'm holding you. The rest of the box is for our movie night.

You should get this box Friday, so Friday night I want you to go and get your slush, pop that popcorn, and watch Poetic Justice. Start the movie at seven. I'll be watching it at my place too. It won't be as good as watching it with you, but it will do for now.

Now onto your previous letter.

So you write fuck books, huh? What's your pen name? I want to check you out. You said you write like you know something that you actually don't. Are you a virgin? Or just inexperienced? Have you never been satisfied? Let me ease your mind... whatever the case... I'm going to make you cum. Repeatedly. Not only will you reach the final destination, but the journey to get there will be amazing, beloved.

In all honesty... I think you being a writer is dope as hell. How many men can say that their wife is an author? That's dope as hell, baby. I know I can't really say that because you write under a pen name, but just knowing that I have this beautiful creative woman at my side... I'm so happy you're mine.

I have no problem with you keeping your cottage. Maybe it can be our little getaway cove. On the weekends we can go there and disconnect from the world. That is... if you want to share that space with me. If not, that's fine too.

I can't wait to cater to you, girl. I think it's pretty fly that you're a girly girl. Your energy will complement mine perfectly. I'm the type of man that wants to spoil my woman, so from this point forward all of your manicures and pedicures will be on me. Whatever the hell else you do will be too.

Tell me what your ideal date would be. Dinner and a movie? Time out on the lake? How can I please you? I'm laidback. I don't go to clubs and parties and shit, but if you want to we can. I'd be more than happy just chilling at the crib watching movies with you. Of course I'm going to take you out and show you off, but I'm selfish. Most times I'll want you all to myself.

I can't believe you're a fighter. As gorgeous as you are I just can't see that but it makes sense. As beautiful as you are I can see you having some haters and needing to handle that shit. Let me assure you — you will never have to worry about me and other women. I will never do anything to make you feel disrespected or insecure. No flirting, no cheating, none of that. I can honestly say you're all that I want, Haylo.

I think it's cute that you sleep with my picture. I sleep with yours too. Stare at it all fucking day. There's nothing that you can say or do to scare me away. I'm yours. Damn. I really don't want to stop writing. This is the only way I have to be connected to you and I don't want to stop. I miss you.

Maarz

Ugh I miss him too! We have like a month and two weeks left to go. I don't know if I'll be able to make it! It wouldn't be as bad if I didn't honestly like him and feel connected to him already but I do. Tears were welling up in my eyes as I stood and went to my office. I needed to write him back. Right now.

To my husband,

Maarz, I don't know how much more of this I can take. I miss you so much. Hearing your voice fucked with me. It made you real. It made this real. Now you do this sweet shit and almost send me over the edge. How are we supposed to go a whole month and two weeks? Write me every day. Every day.

My phone rang and jumbled up my thoughts. There was no point in me hoping it was Maarz as I returned to the living room because I knew it wouldn't be. I picked my phone up and smiled softly at the sight of my mother's picture.

"Hey, Momma," I spoke, sitting in the center of my couch.

"Hey, ladybug. What's wrong?"

"Nothing."

"Don't lie to me. I hear it in your voice. Tell momma what's wrong."

With my elbow on my thigh, I palmed my forehead and massaged my temples.

"I guess it's not anything that's really wrong. I just... I like Maarz a lot more than I expected to and these letters and his packages are starting to feel like torture. I really want to be with him, Momma. I feel so crazy wanting a man this much that I don't even really know but I do. I..." I chuckled quietly and shook my head in disbelief, "I feel like..."

"Like you're starting to love him?"

I nodded as a tear slid down my cheek. The hell was wrong with me? This kind of stuff didn't happen in real life. How could I possibly be this attached to a man I'd just learned of two weeks ago? A man I'd never seen. A man whose voice I only heard once.

"Yes, am I crazy?"

"Why would you think that makes you crazy? Ladybug, Crimson Trails does things the way we do for a very specific reason. Yes, we arrange marriages to make sure the right families align. To make sure our town continues to prosper and be fruitful. To keep power where it needs to be. But we also arrange marriages because marriage is a holy thing here. It is not to be rushed into or taken lightly.

In other places people fall in lust more than anything. They have sex and blind themselves to a person's true character. They get into relationships with people they can't even relate to. All because they're basing their choice of a mate on how they look, how much money they have, or how that person makes them feel.

When parents choose mates for their children we take into consideration things you won't be able to because you're not in a place of clarity all the time in relationships. When you meet someone that you're attracted to and really like, you can be blinded by your feelings. Kind of like... an on the outside looking in thing.

There are things that must be considered before going into marriage that not all young people are able to consider. There are some that are wise and use their common sense. Then there are others who just... rush into things and don't think the important things through.

We ask that the betrothed couple not talk and see each other because we don't want looks and lust to interfere with you growing a genuine connection. These two months are meant to give you the time to really see inside of Maarz. To get to know him with nothing standing in the way of that. These two months are meant to lay a foundation of God and friendship that your marriage will be able to stand on.

It's perfectly normal to want to see him and spend time with him. That means we picked for you well. That means you're gaining a genuine connection with him. But I urge you, Haylo, wait it out."

By now my face was soaked with tears. I'd have to start my letter over. If there was one thing I'd learned about Maarz it was that he was a rule breaker. A rule breaker who had no problem giving me what I wanted. I didn't want to be a negative influence on him and have him coming to see me just because of the tinge of desperation in my letter to see him.

If we were going to do this, we were going to do this right.

No matter how hard and infuriating not having him was.

MAARZ

God smiled on us. A month into our betrothal Crimson Trails newspaper wanted to do an article on Henry & Sons. Guess who they were going to send to do the interview? Haylo. My pops didn't tell me until this morning, and since then I've been pacing in front of the office waiting for her to arrive. He also told me to make sure I didn't touch her in any way. Now that was something I couldn't promise him, but I gave him my word that I'd try.

I was starting to love this girl.

Seriously.

I could literally feel her and hear her as I read her letters, and with each letter we grew closer and closer. So close I felt like I'd known her all of my life. Like she was a part of me that had been missing but was now returned.

The second I saw a blur of pink heading towards the door my pacing stopped. I looked up and out of the door. Sure enough... it was her.

Damn.

That's mine.

My wife. My beloved. My halo.

The pink knee length dress she had on accentuated her curves in such a way that I couldn't wait to find out what her body looked like underneath.

Her hair was a little longer than it was in her picture as it blew in the wind.

When she was close enough to the door to notice that it was me standing at it she hung her head and smiled. Then she stopped walking. Her hands covered her face, and her shoulders began to shudder. Was she crying at the sight of me?

After opening the door, I pulled her inside of it and into my arms.

"Please don't cry, Haylo. *Please* don't cry."

Her arms wrapped around my neck. She tugged me down to her as best as she could and hugged me just as close and tightly as I hugged her. When Haylo's crying slacked up I took her cheeks into my hands and pulled her head out of my chest. I'd waited for this moment. Thought of all the sweet, charming shit I could say. None of that mattered as I looked into her eyes.

"I have to reapply my makeup," she almost whispered with a small smile.

I wiped the tears from her cheeks as my jaw clenched. Not kissing her was going to be the death of me.

"You look beautiful, beloved. You *are* beautiful."

The tips of her fingers slid down my cheek. Over my lips. I couldn't take it anymore. My lips were on hers before I could stop myself, and the way she wrapped her hands around my neck and squeezed let me know she didn't mind. With two handfuls of her ass, I pulled her deeper into my chest. Haylo moaned into my mouth as she opened hers – giving me access to her tongue.

"Dammit, Maarz, I told you no touching," my pops scolded.

He grabbed the back of my shirt and damn near yanked me away from her. That was about the only way I was going to stop. He was talking, but I wasn't hearing shit he was saying. The only thing that was registering in my brain was Haylo as she smiled widely and ran her fingers through her hair.

"Get it together or this is going to be a Henry and one son interview. We can do it without you. Don't do that again," I heard.

That had me giving him my attention. There was no way in hell he was going to keep me from taking advantage of her closeness. I was going to do the interview just to be in the same room as her.

"My fault, Pops. Won't happen again."

He walked over to Haylo and introduced himself, but she was looking at me the whole time he talked. I looked her body over once more before walking over to them.

"Bryson is already in my office. We won't take up too much of your time," he told her as he placed his hand at the top of her back and led her to his office.

"Oh, I don't mind. Like at all."

To keep from smacking her ass I crossed my arms over my chest and followed a few feet behind them. I have never wanted a woman more than I want her in my life. I don't know if it was the fact that I knew she had never had an orgasm before, or because she was so damn sexy, or because I wanted to experience her on every level... but I wanted Haylo. Something serious.

We made it to his office and he sat at his desk. Haylo sat in the middle of me and Bryson. She asked the both of them questions, and I can't tell you a word of what any of them said. I was too busy staring at her gorgeous ass. And when she smiled and laughed... every time she smiled my dick throbbed.

I had to get ahold of myself. The last thing I wanted to do was lust over her so much so that I couldn't even function. I didn't want her to think that sex was all that I wanted from her, but I couldn't help myself. I was about two seconds away from saying fuck the law, picking her up and carrying her to the nearest bathroom, and going deep.

Haylo looked at me and spoke.

"What you say?"

She smiled and licked her lips before repeating herself. Why'd she have to do that? Did she not know that the first place most men looked on a woman's face was her lips?

"I asked if you've always had a passion for money and numbers or was this something you fell into because it's your family's business?"

"I've always been into money and shit. Am I not allowed to curse?"

Haylo smiled again and I swear the sight of her raised cheeks was the most beautiful sight I'd ever seen.

"You can curse. I'll clean it up in the article. Just... talk like you're talking to me."

She asked me about six more questions before she said that was all she needed from us. Pops asked her when he could expect the article to be in the newspaper and that was that. He offered to walk her out but I told him I would.

"Maarz..."

"Ima do right. I won't touch her," I assured him as Bryson chuckled and stood.

"It was very nice meeting you, Haylo. Looking forward to you joining the family."

"Call me Lolo, Bryson. I keep telling you and Mr. Henry that. It was nice to meet you as well."

"Call me Leo, Lolo. Mr. Henry is my father."

Haylo smiled as my pops hugged her.

"Yes, sir. I'm gonna go so you guys can get back to work."

"Thanks again for the interview and feature. And if Maarz tries to get fresh with you outside..."

"Come on, Pops. Cut that out."

I grabbed her hand to lead her out but dropped it quickly. This no touching her thing was going to be a lot harder than I thought. We walked out to her car in silence. I took her keys from her hand and unlocked her door. After giving them back to her I opened the door and stepped away from it to put some space between us.

"It was really good seeing you, baby," I confessed.

"It was good seeing you too. I needed this, Maarz. I feel like I can make these next three weeks now."

I smiled and took a natural step towards her. In three weeks we'd be able to go out on a date. The one and only time we'd be able to see each other again before the wedding. Well, we'd see each other at the rehearsal, but that seemed just as far away.

"Have you found your dress yet?"

Her head shook as she took a step towards me.

"No. I'm going shopping this weekend with my momma and best friends. Hopefully I'll find something and not have to leave town. What about you? You have your tux yet?"

"Nah. Not yet. I'll get it soon."

Her hand slid down my arm until it was enveloped by my hand. I wasted no time intertwining our fingers.

"Leo said you couldn't touch me. He didn't say I couldn't touch you."

"You know what? You're absolutely right. He didn't say you couldn't kiss me either."

I pulled her into me and she lifted herself to kiss my lips. A few pecks in I was sliding my tongue inside of her mouth and grabbing a handful of her hair. She put the other one on my ass and I groaned as I squeezed it. Haylo was a freak.

She was the first to break the kiss, but Haylo didn't move. Her lips were still on mine when she said, "I like you so much. I thought us seeing each other for the first time would be awkward but it feels so..."

"Natural?"

"Exactly."

I put some space between us, just so I'd be able to look into her eyes fully.

"I'm falling for you hard, Haylo. Seeing you further confirms how I've been feeling for you this past month."

Her head hung. She put it in my chest as she hugged me.

"And how do you feel about me, babe?"

"Like I'm falling in love with you," Haylo lifted her head and looked into my eyes, "This ain't even my style. To fall into anything. I'm usually careful. One who takes his time with things. But you... you make me reckless. It's a good reckless, but reckless nonetheless."

"You don't know how long I've been waiting for you to say that. I'm falling in love with you too. It scared me so much at first because I thought it was too soon, but now that I know you feel the same way I feel so much better."

"You should go ahead and go, Haylo. My self-control is being pushed to the max right now and I don't know how much more I can take."

Even with me saying that I was using my body to press hers into the car.

"Okay. Write me tonight?"

"Always."

I kissed her forehead and stepped away. When she was inside of her car I closed the door. After she drove off I made my way back inside of the office. I need a damn drink.

I can still see Maarz's face. His expression when our eyes met. How his shined. How his mouth opened and turned into a smile. Like he was literally taken aback by the sight of me. And what did my silly ass do? Burst into tears! He was so cute trying to comfort me. It was obvious he didn't have a clue what to do with my abrupt display of emotion, but being in his chest... being wrapped in his arms... that was all the comfort I needed.

We agreed that we wouldn't read the last letters we wrote each other until the day we were finally able to go on our date and that was tonight! Well, I don't know if you could really call it a date. I guess it was a date. A supervised date. We'd have our space, but our parents would be in the same building to make sure things didn't get out of hand. I can't lie, I honestly was *not* looking forward to having our every move watched, but I told myself repeatedly that we had to get through this night and our wedding, then we'd have full and complete freedom to be with each other.

Before I started getting ready I slid into the center of my bed in his shirt and read his letter.

Haylo,

Damn woman. I cannot express how much I want you right now. Not just sexually, although I'd be lying if I said I didn't want to make love to you, but I just want you, Haylo. I just want you. I want to be able to hug you. Hold you. Kiss you. Look into your eyes. Those lips. Feel your aura. Enjoy you and have you to myself. I just... want you.

I'm not looking forward to being watched during the one and only time I'll have you before our wedding. Out of respect for our parents and culture I'm going to ride with it. Let me apologize in advance if I'm not able to keep my hands to myself.

I'm trying to think of anything that I won't be able to say when I'm in your presence. You do that to me, you know? Make me speechless. Not so much speechless because I can't think of anything to say, but speechless because my thoughts of you go into overdrive and I can't think of how to express them all at once. I know that words are important to you, so I'll try my best to focus on one thought of you at a time to convey.

Promise you won't overwhelm me in that way that only you can? Promise me that you won't smile. Won't lick your lips. Won't stare into my eyes. Won't speak. Won't touch me. Won't let me hold you. What am I saying? Asking? Not even that would keep me from being consumed by you. I want you to feel just as overtaken by me as I am by you.

That's my goal, Haylo. To slip into every free space in your mind. Your heart. Your soul. Your spirit. Even those places that have taken up space by men of your past. I'm claiming it all. Seeping so deeply inside of you that you feel unlike yourself without me. So deeply that even speaking to another man will make you feel as if you're cheating on me.

You are mine. I want all of you tonight.

See you soon, gorgeous.

Your husband,
Maarz

I placed the letter on my heart, took in a few deep breaths, and got up to get dressed.

I was nervous. So freaking nervous. The entire time I walked to the restaurant I thought the worst. Like what if he doesn't like me when this is over? What if we can't talk face to face? What if the vibe is off? What if one of us says something that the other doesn't like? So much could go wrong… but I needed it to go right. We needed it to go right.

The host opened the door for me and I scanned the dimly lit restaurant. In the far right corner my eyes landed on our parents. My mother waved all happy and proud, causing my father to chuckle and shake his head. I waved back, then motioned with my hands my confusion on where Maarz was. Leo pointed behind me. Slowly, I turned and found who I was looking for.

Maarz was sitting in the opposite corner of the restaurant looking just as good as he wanted to look. He was dressed in white slacks that looked like they were made just for him and a white t-shirt. The blue blazer he had on gave a bit of class to his otherwise casual attire. I couldn't look into his golden eyes like I wanted to because his head was lowered as he looked at his phone, so I inhaled deeply and walked over to him. Trying to look cool and confident because that's certainly not how I felt.

The sound of my heels stabbing the floor gained his attention. Maarz looked up and we locked eyes. He smiled widely and put his phone in his pocket. By the time he stood I was standing in front of him. Taking in his scent. His scent. God that scent. And his eyes. Those golden eyes. His full, pink lips. That stubbly beard. Smooth peanut butter skin. But my attention kept going to his eyes. Swear I could get lost in those eyes.

"Hello, gorgeous."

His left hand wrapped around my waist. He used it to pull me into his chest. Completely ignoring the fact that we weren't supposed to touch each other. No complaints would come from me. I tossed my arms around his neck and hugged him back. Melting into his embrace. Into what felt like where I belonged.

MAARZ

Having her in my arms… that felt like where she belonged. Where I belonged. With her. She matched my fly in a white form fitting skirt that stopped mid-calf. It had a split on the side that gave me a full view of her left leg and half of her thigh. Tucked inside of the high waist skirt was a black see through sheer shirt that matched her black pumps.

Her face was lightly made. Just enough makeup to accentuate her natural beauty. And she had a *lot* of natural beauty. The way her hair swooped over her forehead and covered her eye gave her the sexiest vibe. Between that and those juicy ass gloss covered lips I couldn't help but touch her.

I didn't care who was watching or how much nagging I'd have to hear from my parents. I needed my wife close. Her arms around me and relaxed body against mine let me know she didn't mind at all.

"You look amazing, gorgeous. I'm not going to be able to take my eyes off you the entire night."

Unwillingly, I released her and pulled her seat out.

"Thanks, babe. You look very handsome. Kind of got me nervous," she replied as she sat down.

That got a chuckle out of me while I returned to my seat across from her.

"Nervous? Why?"

"Well I was already nervous about tonight and you look so good I'm just," Haylo shrugged with a smile and sat back in her seat, "It's unnerving. Being around someone so handsome and goodhearted."

"You think I'm goodhearted?"

"I know you are. I know your core is good."

"Look at you. Got me blushing and shit. I think you're dope as hell, Haylo. You have no reason to be nervous because I feel the exact same way that you do. I'm no one to be nervous around. I'm a simple man. The only thing that makes me extraordinary is you."

Haylo smiled a smile that warmed me all over. How could something be so pure and innocent yet have my dick hardening in lust? She had me feeling too many things at once, but that was no surprise. She always had this effect on me. Always had me unable to control my reaction towards her.

The waitress that took my drink order earlier returned to take hers. After ordering what had to be the girliest, sweetest drink on the menu, Haylo asked me...

"Can we switch seats? The sight of our parents making googly eyes over here is creeping me out."

I laughed and stood. Looking around the restaurant, I found a booth that would give us a bit more privacy. And it would allow me to sit closer to her. I went over to the bar and asked our waitress if it was cool for us to switch seats. I didn't want to mess up her rotation. With her permission, I led Haylo over to the booth.

She scooted inside first and I sat as close to her as I possibly could. In this position she wouldn't be able to see our parents at all, and I would only see them if I turned around completely.

"Better?" I asked picking up the menu.

"Much. Thank you."

"So how was your day, gorgeous? You looking forward to the weekend?"

"It was good. Very productive. I am looking forward to the weekend actually. We're going to Chicago so I can look for a dress. I found a boutique online that had some really cute pieces. I can't find anything here."

"That's what's up, babe. I'm sure you'll find something there. Whatever you choose will be good enough for me."

"Do you even care? Like is that something guys care about?"

I put the menu down and looked her over.

"You could walk down the aisle in sweats and my t-shirt for all I care, Haylo, just as long as you're walking down the aisle to *me*."

Her smile. She hit me with that smile again as she placed her hand on top of mine. I flipped it over and entwined our fingers. The second I lifted it to my mouth to kiss it and watched as her eyes closed my phone vibrated in my pocket. I didn't have to look at it to know it was my father telling me to ease up, but I wouldn't. I couldn't. This would be the last time I saw her until our wedding rehearsal. I had to take full advantage of this moment.

"That was really sweet, Maarz. You're going to get us in trouble."

The laughter in her voice made it clear that she didn't care, but I released her hand anyway.

"I'll take all the blame. I apologized in advance if I wouldn't be able to keep my hands to myself…"

"You did. You did. Does it seem like I care?"

She took my hand back into hers and I smiled.

Our waitress returned with her drink and took our orders. I kept it simple with steak and potatoes. Haylo ordered fettuccine.

Haylo took a sip of her drink as I asked her to, "Tell me things."

"Like what?"

"Like… how long you plan on working before you decide to stay at home with our kids. How many kids you plan on carrying for me. How soon you're going to let me get you pregnant."

With a shake of her head Haylo giggled.

"I guess we do have to talk about those things, huh? I mean… I don't know. I don't think I'll ever stop writing books, but I could stop working at the newspaper and magazine whenever you wanted me to. I've always seen myself as this… stay at home wife and mother who writes while the kids are at school and my husband is at work. And when they return home I give all of my time and attention to them. I would like to have you to myself for at least a year, but after that we can have kids. How many do you want? I want two."

"Two is perfect."

Her smile softened as she asked, "You have any goals for the next few years? Anything about your life you want to change?"

"I do. I want to expand Henry & Sons. We make good money because practically everyone in town uses us, but there's only so much that we can do here. I want to open offices in neighboring cities, and eventually go nationwide. Do you want to stay here forever, Haylo? I gotta be honest with you… this is not where I'm trying to live and die."

"I'm following you wherever you go. Whenever you want to go."

The statement itself was profound enough, but the weight of her tone and seriousness in her eyes put me on a whole other level.

"I know we were matched because our parents feel as if we fit each other perfectly, but I need to hear it come out of your mouth. Tell me what you expect from me as your husband. What you offer me as my wife."

"I expect you to love me. Lead me. Make me better. Provide for me. Protect me. Give me the time and affection... the attention I need... to show me that you value me. That I'm a priority to you."

"Done."

"What do you expect from me?"

"I expect you to respect me. Submit to me. Love me. Influence me to be better. Help me reach the vision I have for us and our family. Appreciate me and let me know that you appreciate all that I do for you. Because I'm going to spoil you, Haylo. Give you your every want and need. All I ask is that you remain loyal and faithful to me."

We stared at each other for a few seconds before she told me all that she had to offer me as a woman. As my wife. As the mother of my children. I in return told her what I had to offer her. By the time we were done our food arrived. We ate in a pretty comfortable silence. Sharing our food... well... I shared my shit with her, but all she offered me was the broccoli out of her pasta because she didn't like it. Crazy ass.

After dinner we headed to Creamed for dessert. The joy that covered her face from something as simple as an ice cream slush made me want to give her the world.

"What do you like about me?" she asked as we walked down the street side by side.

I wrapped my free arm around her shoulder and pulled her closer to me. Our parents were walking behind us with enough distance between us to make Haylo comfortable.

"I like everything that I know about you. I like your passion. Your heart. Your creativity. Your beauty. Your silliness. Your spunk. Your loyalty to this crazy process. The love and respect you have for your parents to even be going through with this. I like everything about you, beloved. I love you."

Her feet stopped moving. Haylo turned to the side and looked up at me.

"What did you say?"

"I said I like everything about you."

She smiled and pushed me softly.

"After that."

"Your beauty?"

"*After* that."

"Your loyalty?"

"After that, babe!"

"I love you. I'm committed to growing in love with you for the rest of my life. To telling you and showing you. Getting to know you through our letters allowed me to see you in a way that I've never seen a woman before. I saw you. Past your beauty. Past feelings. Past attraction. I saw *you*. I love you, Haylo."

Her lips parted as she looked back at our parents before hugging my neck, then wrapping her arms around my stomach and pulling me closer. We held each other long enough for what I'd said to sink in. Haylo lifted her head, still in my arms, and said...

"I'm so happy they chose you. I'm happy you're taking me. I love you, Maarz."

Not giving a damn about rules, I lowered myself to her and kissed her. I'd deal with the consequences later. For now... this was what we both wanted and needed. This closeness. And I wasn't going to let anything or anyone rob us of this moment. Especially when she pulled away only to sit her slush down before returning her lips to mine.

Haylo

A few days after our date it was time for us to have our separate give away parties. That's right. Give away. Our parents hosted parties for us that symbolized the act of them giving us away. Kind of like an *even though you're grown as hell I'm finally recognizing you as an adult and cutting the umbilical cord* kind of thing. After this, we'd have one big party that we both could attend. It would be after the only wedding rehearsal we'd have. Then it was going to be time for the real thing. The real thing. As in us getting married. *Married.*

Sometimes I wake up and still can't believe this is my life. Like, not only am I getting married soon… but it's to a man that I absolutely adore. I know the real test will come after our wedding when we start living together, but I can't wait to get to know Maarz on that level! I can't think of anything that he could say or do to tarnish the perception of him I've gained through his letters.

While I waited for my besties to arrive for the party, I helped my mother with the last of the cooking she had to do. Well I tried to help, but all she would allow me to do was carry the trays from the kitchen to the dining room. I couldn't even set the dishes up and make them look pretty.

As I made my way to the dining room with the bowl of rotel that I was definitely about to sneak into my little sister, Leigha, grabbed my arm and told me to meet her outside when I was done. She had a look of bewilderment on her face that would've alarmed me had I not already known how much of a little drama queen she could be.

After putting a scoop of rotel on two tortilla chips I headed outside to find Leigha pacing back and forth on the porch.

"What's wrong, Lei?" I asked before popping one of the chips in my mouth.

"I just... why are you doing this, Lolo? Are you seriously going through with this? I cannot *believe* you're going through with this," she stopped talking but I didn't answer. Leigha was longwinded. I'm sure there was more that she wanted to say. I ate the other chip while I waited and sure enough after inhaling a deep breath she continued, "Why didn't you leave when you turned 18? I'm not sticking around for them to force a man on me. I'm taking my own path. Finding my own love. This is crazy, Lolo. Crazy."

"I felt that way when I was your age, but when I turned 18 I just... didn't want to leave. Not only is all of my family and my friends here, but I felt a tug that told me to stay. Like I'd be missing out on something if I left. Now I know that that something was actually someone. It was Maarz. Had they chosen any man other than him I probably would be freaking out and regretting staying, but Maarz is... everything, Lei. I really do love him."

"How?! How do you love him, Lolo? You don't even know him. Y'all haven't even had sex yet! What if he sucks in bed? You're going to spend the rest of your life with a man who's lousy in bed."

With a chuckle I put my hands together as if I was praying and put them over my mouth.

"First of all... the hell do you know about sex, little girl? What you know about any man being good or bad at it?"

"That's beside the point..."

"Secondly, do you really think sex and love are the same thing? Do you think you can't love someone that you haven't had sex with?"

"Well... they *do* call it making love..."

"But that's not true. That's not meant to be taken literally. Here..." I pointed towards the step needed to get off the porch, "Sit down."

We sat down and I tackled all of her problems with me and Maarz one by one.

"I appreciate you looking out for me, Leigha, but I'm confident that Maarz is the man for me. He's my soul mate. That's how I love him. We connected at the soul through our letters. We've gotten to know the facts about each other. Our fears. Our strengths and weaknesses. Our goals and dreams. Visions. What we love and hate.

We've bared our souls to each other and become friends before anything. It was good that we didn't spend time with each other when we first started because we're so attracted to each other that we probably would've had sex and ruined anything we could've had because we rushed into it.

We wouldn't have taken the time to get to know each other and what we need and want in order for our relationship to work. Maarz isn't perfect and neither am I. There are things that he needs me to do during our marriage that I probably wouldn't have known about had we not taken things as slow as we have, just like there are things that I need from him that had we had sex first I probably wouldn't have thought to discuss with him.

This is the deal, mama, men and women both have power. For men, their power is in commitment. For women, our power is in pus— it's in our sex. Not all men are as well-mannered and respectful as the men here in Crimson Trails. There are some men that will cater to you and treat you like a Queen until you give them what they want… sex… then leave you. There are some men that will lie to you and tell you they want love and commitment but don't. Then there are some men who may want those things… just not with you. And you could find a man who wants those things with you and it just doesn't work.

The only things that help you be sure of a man's true intentions are time and his energy. The vibe you get from him. Vibes never lie. He might try to fake it… but the vibe you get from him will never lie. The best way to know if a man is serious about you is to hold off on sex; especially if he hasn't committed to you. Once you tie that soul tie it will be hard to let him go if things don't work out.

So without me being around Maarz and having sex with him, I was able to see the real him. The inside of him. I fell in love with him. With his heart. His genuineness. Now when we get together our relationship is going to be solid because we have friendship to stand on.

Some couples do nothing but go out on dates and have sex because they don't have anything in common. They're not friends. They can't relate. That won't be the case with the man chosen for you. I will never talk you into staying here because everyone has to go down their own path. All I can say is follow your heart, but make sure you take your mind with you and think it through.

And as far as sex is concerned, I'm pretty confident that that won't be an issue. Even if it was we'll have our entire lives to figure out how to please each other."

"I guess. If I stay... and I'm not saying I'm staying... I'm going to leave... but if I stay... I hope they pick a man as fine as Maarz for me. All of what you just said won't mean nothing if he's ugly and that's real."

"Leigha! Looks aren't everything. If he's fine and treats you like shit then what? It's okay to want a good looking man, but that's not what's most important. And that's not to say that unattractive men to you will give you what you deserve. You never can say about those kinds of things. Just gotta... be wise. Protect your heart and be wise."

She nodded and I could tell none of what I was saying was registering in her closed off mind. Leigha might not have wanted to stay home and let our parents choose her husband, but she needed to. There was nothing but trouble waiting for her if she left. She was way too close minded and open and loose in other ways to not experience a life of pain when it came down to men.

"I hear you, Lolo. If you're happy that's all that matters. I fuck with myself more than anybody else, so I assure you... me getting played by a man for sex will *never* happen."

"Watch your mouth."

"I'll be 18 in three days; you might as well get used to it."

"Whatever. I'm not about to play with you and get my pressure up."

We went back inside and I was so happy to see that Trevena and Chrisette had arrived. I didn't care about anybody else making it. I had everyone here that I needed now. Everyone except Maarz, and he wouldn't be in attendance. My thoughts of him would have to carry me through. As freaking usual.

"We're about to head out, ladybug. You need anything before we go?" my mother asked as she stood over me.

The last of the guests had finally left and I was more than happy for the peace and quiet. In fact, I'd gone to my room just to get a break from all of the noise. Sure it was happy noise... loud talking and laughing with those closest to each other, but I just needed a break.

"Nah, I'm good, Momma. Thanks for everything."

She nodded as she stroked my hair softly.

"I'm proud of you, Haylo. I love you so much."

"I love you too."

"I have something for you. It's..."

"My last letter?"

I sat up straight as she went into her purse.

It was customary that all letters stop after the date. They felt you'd have enough to think and pine over just from being in each other's presence. The final one was to be given by the parents at the give away party. In just days I'd be in his presence again. I'd be his wife. But until then... this last letter would be all I'd have.

"Your last letter."

She handed it to me... and for the longest time all I could do was look at it while she looked at me.

"Well... come lock the door behind us so you can get to reading."

Clutching the letter tightly, I followed her out of my room to the front door. After giving them all hugs, I locked up behind them and headed to the center of my couch to get comfortable and read.

Baby,

In one of the previous letters you wrote me you asked me why I have so many nicknames for you. With this being the last letter you'll get from me I figured this would be the best time to tell you. I explained why you were my halo in my first letter to you. I call you baby because that's what you are. My baby. Not in the sense of being a child; but there's an innocence about you and childlike trust in me and my ability to take care of you that causes me to want to spoil you and cater to you.

I call you beloved because you are my beloved. I treasure you. You are the woman I want to love and be loved by. I call you gorgeous because, shit just look in the mirror! You are gorgeous, Haylo. I think that's all I call you. What I'm looking most forward to is calling you my wife. We're almost there, baby.

You know what I can't get out of my mind from our date? Just sitting there next to you. I remember riding down Elliot Grove and passing the Pattersons and Johnsons houses. You remember them? They were the oldest couples in Crimson Trails until they died three years ago. What was so crazy was that they all died right after each other.

Mrs. Patterson died first and then Mr. Patterson died two months later. The next year Mr. Johnson died and Mrs. Johnson died less than a week later. They taught me one thing in that moment — love is real. So is heartache. You can literally die from a broken heart. That pain can weigh on you physically so strong that it causes you to lose hope. And without hope... we don't have anything in life.

I didn't understand it then how they could just sit on their front porches all day doing nothing. Sometimes I'd ride by and they would be talking to each other, but for the most part they'd be sitting there in complete silence. Just sitting there next to each other watching cars and people go by. I couldn't understand how they could find any pleasure in that.

It makes sense now. When you're with the person you love the activity doesn't matter. You could literally be sitting on a porch doing nothing for hours and still have the small hint of a satisfied smile they had. The kind of satisfied smile that comes from being with the one you love.

I can't wait to grow old with you. I can't wait to do nothing with you. I can't wait to spend the rest of my life loving you.

Your husband,
And babe
Maarz

I didn't realize I was crying until one of the tears hit the paper. Immediately holding the letter away from it as not to ruin it, I wiped my face of the happy tears and sighed. And prayed. That one day Leigha and every other woman would experience the kind of love that I am because of Maarz. The kind of love that can't be understood unless you experience it yourself. The kind of love that you can't explain because really... how can you explain a feeling that you've never felt before? How do you explain what it feels like to be free yet bound to a person at the same time? How?

MAARZ

I knew I shouldn't be here, but as soon as my give away party was over I found myself sitting outside of Haylo's cottage with her letter in my hand. Every letter that she'd written me up until this point made me feel something. Whether it was happiness and laughter, love, deep need, lust... I've always felt *something* from reading her feelings. This last one, though, this last one made me feel something I'd never felt before – aching.

Aching.

Sorrow.

Distress.

Pain.

Not because she said anything bad, but because of the love and goodness that she poured into the letter. It made me ache for her. Literally ache for her.

I tried to will myself to leave. To convince myself that this closeness was as close as I needed to get, but I still found myself opening the door and walking up to hers. The second I rang the doorbell I turned to leave, but by the time I'd made it to her mailbox she was calling my name. I didn't turn around to face her. If I saw her I wouldn't be able to leave. There was still a chance for me to continue walking away, but that would be over if I turned around and saw her face.

"Is something wrong, Maarz? Are you okay?"

"I'm fine. Everything's fine. Read your letter."

"Oh. You wanna come in?"

"I don't think that's a good idea, beloved. I shouldn't even be here."

"True, but when has that ever stopped you?"

I smiled as I turned around slowly to face her. Haylo was smiling as well. Even in basketball shorts and a t-shirt... *my* t-shirt... she was still the most beautiful woman I'd ever seen.

"Take a walk with me. By the lake."

"Okay. Let me grab my shoes. I'll meet you down there."

With a nod, I made my way behind her cottage to the lake. My hands were in my pockets to keep myself from touching her, but that didn't stop her from hugging me as soon as she made her way down. After taking her cheeks into my hands I lifted her head from my chest and kissed her forehead.

"You're not changing your mind are you, babe?" she asked, looking up at me with those mesmerizing eyes.

"Of course not. If anything I'm losing my patience to wait for you. To take you."

"Me too. In all of my preparing for this moment I never thought…"

Her lips closed. Head shook. Eyes watered.

"You never thought you'd love a man that was picked for you as much as you do? Never thought you could get so close to someone and yet still be *so* far away?"

"Yes," she whispered, "Will it change? Will *you* change?"

"It will only get better, Haylo. I promise you that."

I wrapped my arms around her. Rested my chin on the top of her head gently. And held her until the sun went down.

Haylo

"I feel like I'm about to throw up," I confessed through my sob — which was making it impossible for Chrisette to do my makeup.

It was the day we'd been waiting for... our wedding day... and I was a nervous wreck! My legs were shaking. Hands were shaking. I couldn't stop crying. Felt like I was about to start hyperventilating. Not because I was starting to second guess marrying Maarz, but because after today my life wouldn't be the same.

I was going to go from my independent life in my cottage where I was closed off from the world until I wanted to come out, to living with someone else. A man. My husband. I was about to be somebody's wife! I don't know anything about being somebody's wife! All I could think about was screwing this whole thing up!

"Come on now, Haylo, aren't you ready to finally be able to be with Maarz?" my mother asked as she wiped my face for what felt like the millionth time.

"Well, yes, but I..."

"No buts. He's waiting for you. This beautiful dress is waiting for you. Stop crying before you make yourself sick, ladybug."

My dress was beautiful. I looked over at it in time enough to see Trevena sneaking out of the door. When she closed it the dress swayed against the door lightly. The moment I saw my dress I knew it was the one. I had to go all the way to Chicago to find the Sevilla Couture gown that I'd been eyeing online.

"Fine. Just... let me have a minute to get myself together."

She stepped back and so did Chrisette. Just that little distance and space made me breathe easier. Maybe that was the problem. Too many women in this room all up in my personal space. I've never liked being around a lot of people at once; that's why I ended up going to my room at my party.

Trevena stepped back in and left the door slightly open, making the room even smaller.

"Lolo, I have somebody behind the door that wants to talk to you."

"Who?" I asked as I stood and wiped the tears my mother couldn't catch.

"Maarz," just the mention of his name made me feel lighter. "Of course he can't come in, but you can talk to him through the door."

I walked over to the door and closed my eyes as I inhaled his scent.

"Maarz?"

"What's wrong, beloved?"

"Nothing. I'm just... scared."

"Of what? You don't want to do this anymore?"

"No. I mean no that's not it. I want to. I just... don't want to mess this up. Mess us up."

"I told you that you didn't have to worry about that..."

"I know. I know."

"Give me your hand," Maarz slid his hand inside of the cracked door. I placed my hand inside of his, "Let's pray."

I closed my eyes and allowed him to lead me in prayer.

"Lord, send out your Spirit. Fill Haylo with your strength and your peace. Allow that peace to wash over her and give her confidence... not in herself... but in your spirit in her. Remind her that she can do and be all things through Christ. Including being a dam– a darn good wife and mother.

I pray that our love for one another be all encompassing and all consuming. Lord, make our love pleasurable. Make it be as creative as it is stable, as passionate as it is respectful, as gentle as it is strong. Let all who know us see in our love the love and hand of you, our creator. If and when we are blessed with children, may they thrive in the passionate and energizing love that has its beginning in the love you have for the world and all its people. In Jesus name we pray and we thank you. Amen."

Maarz pulled my arm further out of the door and kissed my hand.

"Thanks, babe. I really needed that."

"Always. I love you, Haylo."

"I love you."

MAARZ

This was the day I'd been waiting for. The day I was finally able to make Haylo my wife. Weddings here in Crimson Trails weren't like traditional weddings. Not everyone fell for their mates as quickly as me and Haylo fell for each other, so we didn't have traditional weddings here. No traditional vows. No church service with a congregation full of people that we hardly knew. Just each other and those that were genuinely close to us.

All of the weddings were held inside or outside of town square. Depending on the weather and how heavy the wind was blowing the couple could choose to have the wedding inside or outside. Not wanting to risk our candles being blown out because of the wind, Haylo chose to have our wedding inside of the oldest building in town square.

So there I stood. Here I stood. In the ballroom of this dimly lit building waiting for her to make her way to me. Most of the lights were out, but a few remained along with candles that allowed us to see.

It felt like I'd been standing there all my life waiting for her, but the moment my sister in law started singing "At Last" by Etta James I knew she was finally about to make her way to me. Everyone that was in attendance stood and started looking towards the hallway, but Haylo's bridesmaids didn't start walking out until Bridget's singing was replaced with violin playing.

My face may have looked relaxed, but my nervousness was made apparent by the side to side swaying I started doing. Bryson's hand on my shoulder stopped me. I looked over at him and he gave me an understanding look that made me smile. Cameras started flashing. Oohs and aahs filled the room.

She was here.

I looked forward and sure enough... there was my bride. My *beautiful* bride. I watched her walk to me and all I could do was think about how empty I was before her. How full her and her letters had made me. How loving my life was about to be because of her. How she was about to be mine for the rest of my life. And before I could stop them... tears were falling as I shook my head.

What did I do to deserve her?

I looked over at Bryson to ask him, but his ass was shedding a tear on my behalf too. Inhaling deeply, I brushed my tears away quickly before Haylo made her way in front of me completely. She still saw them, though. Had a few of her own falling. I wiped her face as she wiped mine with a smile.

After kissing her forehead, I took her hand into mine and put her at my side. My left side. Close to my heart. Where she belonged as my returned rib.

Our parents lit one tapered candle, then prayed a prayer of blessing over our union.

Bryson and her sister Leigha lit their candles, then prayed a prayer of blessing over our union.

The pastor lit his candle, then took both of our hands into his to pray.

"Father in heaven, thank You for this husband, Maarz, and wife, Haylo, and their commitment to marriage. As we look ahead, we pray that their future will never lack the convictions that make a marriage strong.

Bless this husband, Maarz. Bless him as a provider and protector. Sustain him in all the pressures that come with the task of stewarding a family. May he so live that his wife may find in him the haven for which the heart of a woman truly longs.

Bless this wife, Haylo. Give her a tenderness that makes her great, a deep sense of understanding, and a strong faith in you. Give her that inner beauty of a soul that never fades, that eternal youth that is found in holding fast to the things that never age. May she so live that her husband may be pleased to reverence her in the shrine of his heart.

Teach them that marriage is not living for each other. It is two people uniting and joining hands to serve you. Give them a great spiritual purpose in life. May they seek first your kingdom and your righteousness, knowing that you will sustain them through all of life's challenges.

May they minimize each other's weaknesses and be swift to praise and magnify each other's strengths. Bless them and develop their characters as they walk together with you. Give them enough hurts to keep them humane, enough failures to keep their hands clenched tightly in yours, and enough of success to make them sure they walk with you throughout all of their life.

May they never take each other's love for granted but always experience that breathless wonder that exclaims, "Out of all this world, you have chosen me." Then, when life is done and the sun is setting, may they be found then as now, still hand in hand, still very proud, still thanking you for each other.

May they travel together as friends and lovers, brother and sister, husband and wife, father and mother, and as servants of Christ until he shall return or until that day when one shall lay the other into the arms of God. This we ask through Jesus Christ, our Lord and Savior, the great lover of our souls. Amen."

I don't think there was a dry eye in the building after he finished praying, but me and Haylo… our eyes were. Our smiles were content. It was as if we were stepping into that prayer… fully prepared to live and love for the rest of our days.

After that it was time for us to light our own candles and pray together. This prayer was the same prayer every couple had to pray together. I'd been practicing it every day since I found out Haylo had been chosen for me, but no amount of preparation prepared me for this moment as I took her hands into mine.

"Dear God,

We praise you for your love and faithfulness. We thank you for grace. We thank you that you give us the power to love well. Thank you for my spouse. Thank you for the gift of marriage.

Lord, we pray for… adoration. Blessing. Commitment. Endurance. Faithfulness. Forgiveness. Friendship. Generosity. Grace. Humility. Intimacy. Love. Mercy. Oneness. Peace. Respect. Submission. Trust. Understanding. Value. And wisdom. In Jesus name we pray and claim all these things and all else that you have for us through grace. Amen."

We lit the last two candles and chuckled after we both let out a loud sigh.

"By the power vested in me by God and man I now pronounce you man and wife. Maarz, you may now…"

He'd said enough. My arms were around her just as quickly as my lips were on hers.

"I don't want you to feel pressured to give yourself to me tonight, Haylo. We have the rest of our lives for that. Whenever you're comfortable enough and ready to take it there... I don't mind waiting," Maarz assured me as I walked into what would be our bedroom for the next week. We'd been in our rental for all of an hour. The first thing I wanted to do was shower and get out of that dress, but I let him shower first because I knew I'd be in there for a while. After taking a shower under the hottest water I could stand, I allowed my body to marinate in my favorite honey body butter.

Now I was standing at the doorframe in nothing but a towel watching him.

He was sitting on the edge of the bed looking all sexy. Wearing nothing but his boxers, Maarz had taken the time while I was in the bathroom to light a few candles, get some low music going, and sprinkle rose petals all over the floor and bed.

"I just want to hold you," he continued as he stood, "Enjoy having you in my arms."

He started my way, and the second I was within arm's reach Maarz was pulling me into his chest and wrapping his arms around me. After taking his hand into mine I put it between my legs.

"Does it feel like I'm not ready?"

The sight of him biting down on his lip as his fingers slid between my slit...

"Are you sure, baby?"

My head went to the doorframe softly. Between his thumb massaging my clit and his middle finger massaging my insides, I couldn't form a complete thought or sentence. I simply nodded and spread my legs a little wider.

Maarz picked me up and carried me over to the bed. He placed me in the center of it, stepping back only to stare at me.

"Take the towel off," he ordered.

I opened the towel and pulled it from under me, dropping it onto the floor afterwards. For what felt like forever he just stood there... staring at every inch of me. I mean his eyes started at the top of my head and made their way down to my feet. And the entire time he did I could see the print of his dick growing bigger and bigger underneath his boxers.

"I figured your body would be beautiful... but this is more than what I was expecting, beloved. And it's mine?"

"All yours. Show me what's mine."

"Not yet. Let me have you first."

With my arms crossed in protest, I watched as he sauntered over to me.

Maarz made his way between my legs, wrapping them around him in the process. His lips were on mine. Kissing me tenderly. Passionately. Every so often he'd suck my lips into his mouth. Bite down on my bottom lip softly. Spread my lips and connect our tongues. I didn't think I could get any wetter... but kissing my husband had me on the verge of wanting to climax.

His lips started down my neck. Between my chest. Biting my breasts. Soft enough to not hurt. Hard enough to let me feel him there. His tongue swirled around my nipples. Dipping into the center of them until I shivered and pushed him away.

This wasn't my first time... but I'd never had an orgasm with a man before. Call me crazy, but I felt like that was my punishment for not saving myself for my husband. Never being satisfied. I felt like I'd never have a pleasurable sexual experience until it was with my husband, and already Maarz was proving that to be true.

My stomach caved as he licked and kissed it. Filled with butterflies the lower he went. I never liked oral. Never liked the idea or feel of a man gnawing at my pussy. What was so great about that shit? Maarz spread my legs and began to lick, suck, and kiss on my thighs until I was pushing him away. It felt too good. So good it was overwhelming.

He stared at my pussy, just an inch of space between it and him, and licked his lips. He was so close I could feel his breath.

"Maarz... I don't like that," I admitted quietly.

"Let me eat. If you don't like it, I'll stop. But let me eat."

My trust in him and desire to please him had me nodding even though I was sure I wouldn't like it. Maarz slowly began to caress my clit with his tongue. He took my hands into his, probably to keep me from pushing him away, and held me down. His tongue slid over both of my holes, filling my body with warmness – then he focused back on my clit.

Sucking it into his mouth. Pulling it out only to circle his tongue around it. Up and down. Side to side.

Then he'd lap up the cream that was spilling out of me.

I was doing fine until he hardened the tip of his tongue against the top of my clit. That was my undoing. My moans began to pour out of me without my control. Biting down on my lip didn't stop them from erupting in my throat. And when he sucked my clit back into his mouth and slid his finger inside of me I moaned loudly as my walls clutched him.

As they pulsed. As my legs trembled. As I came. For the first time in my life. Off his tongue and finger on top of that!

Maarz dried my cum and made me wet all over again before lifting himself and asking, "Still don't like it?" with a smile.

I shook my head no and smiled myself as he got out of the bed.

"No. I love it."

"That's *my* pussy. She belongs to me just as much as you do. *That's* why nobody has ever made her cum before. That's my job."

He handled his job well too. So well my eyes were lowering I was so relaxed. I could've gone straight to sleep, but Maarz pulled his boxers down and the sight of his dick definitely gave me a jolt of energy.

"Maarz…"

"Changing your mind?"

Maarz crawled back between my legs, brushing his long, curved dick against my clit. And it was thick. It was perfect. Just perfect. From the way it was a tab bit darker than his skin at the top of his shaft, to the way the veins that lined it curved as they stretched towards the head. It was beautiful. So beautiful I wanted to taste it, but before I could he was rubbing it against my clit. Covering it with the cream he'd left there.

"Can I have it now, babe? *Please?*"

There was no shame in my game. I wanted to feel all of him inside of me. Like *right* now.

Slowly he pressed his way inside of me, grabbing my thighs and keeping them from closing until he was all the way inside of me. Maarz lowered himself and kissed me. Being ever the gentleman and giving me time to adjust to him. When he felt like I was ready, Maarz lifted himself and pulled out of me. Sliding back in just as slow. But even more deep. Each time he pulled out he was slicker from my wetness.

"Shit, Maarz," I moaned, feeling my insides heat.

His grip on my thighs tightened as my legs began to close involuntarily. My hands went to his chest… trying to push him away… but that didn't work. I didn't *want* it to work. I wanted him to continue to dig inside of me. Continue to make my pussy leak.

What was he doing to me?

"You gotta get used to this dick, huh? Just lay there and take it, baby. Let me make you feel good."

That only heightened my arousal. My heat. My wetness. My walls tightened against him and he moaned himself. The sight of my cream drenching his dick had me in awe. I'd never seen anything like it before. Never known of a person having such control over someone else before. He was literally pulling me out of myself.

Literally inside of me.

Literally connected to me.

It was all too much.

My legs started trembling again and this time I was struggling to hold my orgasm off.

"You not gon do it?" he asked – his voice husky and laced with lust, "You not gon cum?"

Maarz released my thighs and allowed me to wrap them around him. He lowered himself to me and kissed me. Stroked me a little faster. A little harder. A little deeper. Just until my back was arching off the bed and I bit down on his bottom lip as I came.

His movements stopped and he watched as I came against him. Pussy pulsing. Legs falling as limp as cooked linguine. He waited. Waited until I came down.

As soon as I did tears rained from my eyes. Had I had any doubt that Maarz was the man for me the act of us becoming one… the consummation of our marriage… the fact that he was so in tune with my body… causing something no man ever could before… this confirmed it. This confirmed that he was the man for me.

He kissed my tears away before covering my lips with his. I took his cheeks into my hands and stared into his eyes.

"You're really mine. This is really real. This isn't a dream? Maarz… you're really my husband."

"I am. And you're really my wife," he rocked his hips against mine, "My baby," he lifted himself slightly and rubbed my clit as he stroked me again, "My *gorgeous* baby," and again. Taking my breath away. Replacing it with quivering lips that opened and couldn't close, "My beloved," and again. Gave me my breath back. New life. With him. My nails dug into his thighs as the pressure building up within me intensified, "My halo."

His declarations. The love in his eyes. Passion in his voice. Thumb on my clit. Strokes hitting every inch and crevice of me. I wasn't running away this time. If anything I wanted more. Pulling him back down to me, I wrapped my arms around his neck as he buried his face inside of my neck.

"Maarz… can I… have…"

"You want more… don't you?"

"Yessss."

Maarz hooked the back of my knees between his arms. Spread my legs as wide as they could go. Pushed them into the bed. Grabbed two handfuls of my hair. Filled me to the hilt. Over and over again. Each stroke deeper. Harder. Faster. Each stroke snatching my breath. My moans. Each stroke numbing my body, yet sensitizing me to feel nothing but him. Nothing but him. All over me.

Suddenly the bedroom was no longer filled with just the knocking headboard, our heavy breathing, my cream slathering his dick, and his guttural moans. My moans returned. And so did my panting. And my voice as I moaned his name.

This time when I came my legs didn't shake. No. They locked completely. Just like my walls locked against him. Just as my back arched and froze midair. This time when I came he came with me. Stopping his movements completely. In fact, the only things that continued to move was his chest as he regulated his breathing and his dick throbbing inside of me. Filling me with his seeds as he let out the sexiest moan and laid on top of me.

I caressed his back, smiling at the slurs seeping from his lips.

"Haylo?"

"Yea, babe?"

"I love you."

"You do?"

"I do."

I kissed his cheek. He kissed my lips.

"I love you too."

We stayed like that. Him inside of me. Between my legs. On my chest. With me caressing his back. For I don't know how long. Long enough for him to fall asleep and start snoring softly. Funny thing is… for the *first* time in my life… being here with him… I felt airy. I felt awake. I felt… alive.

THE END.

62375924R00032

Made in the USA
Lexington, KY
06 April 2017